Explore the World of
Space and the Universe

Text by Iain Nicolson
Illustrated by Sebastian Quigley

A GOLDEN BOOK • NEW YORK
Western Publishing Company, Inc., Racine, Wisconsin 53404

© 1992 Ilex Publishers Limited. Printed in Spain. All rights reserved. No part of this publication may be
reproduced in any form without the prior written permission of the copyright owner. All trademarks are
the property of Western Publishing Company, Inc. Library of Congress Catalog Card Number: 92-70500
ISBN: 0-307-15608-7/ISBN: 0-307-68608-6 (lib.bdg.) A MCMXCII

Contents

What is the _Freedom_ space station?
Orbiting high above the Earth, space station _Freedom_ will be a permanently manned research center and a base for missions to the Moon, Mars, and beyond. Laboratories and living quarters will be attached near the center of a long frame. Solar panels at each end will convert sunlight into electrical power.

Why can we see the Horsehead nebula?

The Horsehead nebula in the constellation Orion is a dark cloud of dust, shaped like a horse's head and mane, that shows up against a more distant, glowing gas cloud. Huge clouds of thinly spread gases (mainly hydrogen) and tiny dust particles exist in the depths of space. If a cloud contains some very hot, bright stars, the energy emitted, or given off, by these stars causes the gases to shine. A glowing gas cloud is called an emission nebula. When a cold, dusty cloud—like the Horsehead nebula—lies in front of an emission nebula or a background of stars, it blocks out light and shows up as a dark patch.

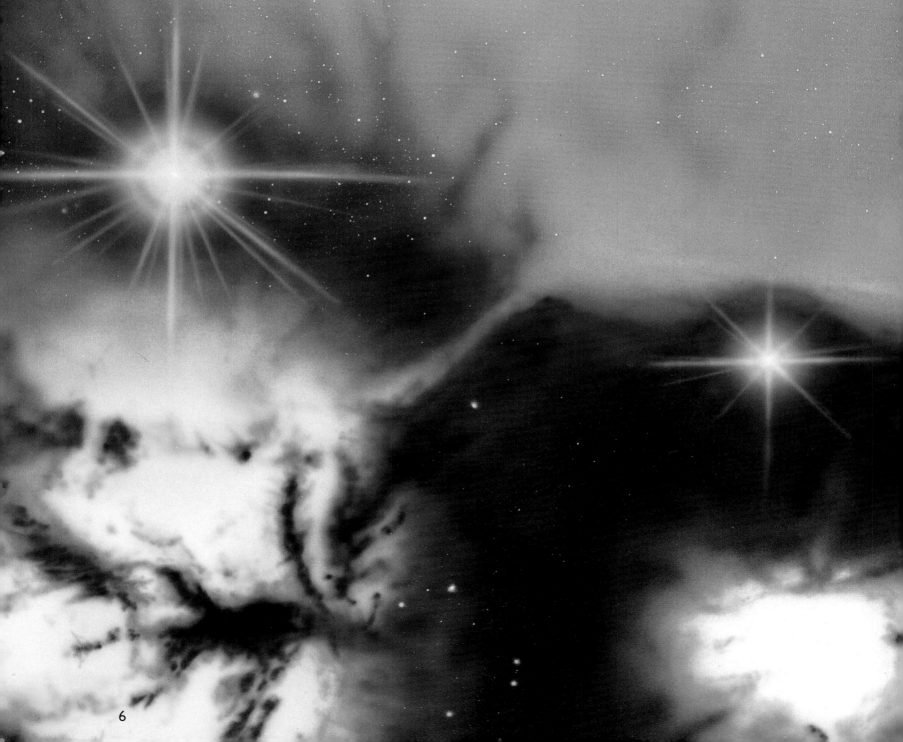

The Crab nebula is a supernova remnant, the debris of a star that blew itself apart in a colossal explosion seen by Chinese observers in the year 1054. Despite its great distance of 6,000 light-years from Earth, the exploding star was bright enough to be seen in daylight for a few weeks that year.

The Orion nebula is a huge cloud of gases lit up by 4 very hot, young stars, which are known as the Trapezium. The nebula is located in the "sword" of Orion, south of Orion's "belt." It can be seen with the naked eye on a clear, dark night and can easily be seen with binoculars.

What is the Milky Way galaxy?

The Milky Way galaxy is a huge island of about 100,000 million stars. Many of them are packed into the nucleus, or central bulge. This is surrounded by a thin, flat circle, or disk, containing more stars, gas clouds, and dust that are arranged in a spiral pattern measuring 100,000 light-years across. (A light-year is the distance traveled by light in a year—about 6 trillion miles.) The Sun *(shown by the red square)* is an ordinary star that lies about 30,000 light-years from the center of the galaxy. The universe contains billions of galaxies of different shapes and sizes. The most distant ones are so far away, their light has taken 10 billion years to reach us.

More about galaxies

Seen from the Earth, the Milky Way looks like a faint band of starlight stretching across the sky. It is made up of the combined light of millions and millions of stars which, like the Sun, lie in the disk of our galaxy. The Milky Way can be seen on a clear, dark night.

The three main galaxy types are: spiral, elliptical, and irregular. Spiral galaxies, like the Milky Way, have a central nucleus surrounded by a spiral-shaped disk. They contain gases and dust from which new stars are formed. Elliptical galaxies range in shape from spheres to flattened ovals and contain little, if any, gases. Irregular galaxies, which have no particular shape, contain mostly young stars, gases, and much dust.

What is the Solar System?

The Solar System consists of the Sun, nine planets, and numerous comets, meteoroids, and asteroids. In order of average distance from the Sun, the planets are: Mercury, Venus, Earth, Mars (the terrestrial planets); Jupiter, Saturn, Uranus, Neptune (the giant planets); and Pluto, which follows a strange orbit. The Earth takes a year to travel around the Sun. Mercury speeds around the Sun in just 88 days, while distant Pluto takes nearly 248 years to complete each circuit. Most of the planets in the Solar System have satellites, or moons, that travel around them.

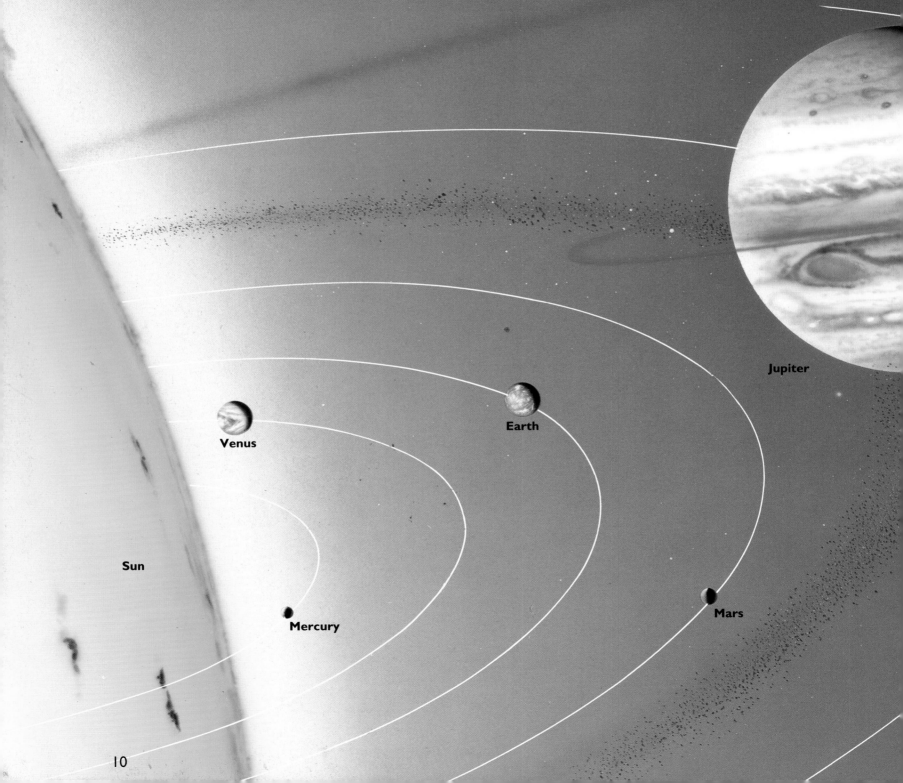

Sun

Mercury

Venus

Earth

Mars

Jupiter

Uranus

Neptune

Pluto

Saturn

11

Why is the Sun so bright?

The Sun is our nearest star. Like any other star, it is a huge globe of hot gases that pours light, heat, and energy into space. Although it is 93 million miles away, it still appears with a dazzling brightness in the daytime sky. Its diameter, or width, of 865,000 miles is more than a hundred times larger than the Earth's. Dark cooler patches, called sunspots, often appear on the Sun's surface. Sometimes violent explosions, called solar flares, erupt close to sunspots. Huge streamers of hot gases, called prominences, surge up and down, occasionally reaching heights of hundreds of thousands of miles. Others seem to hang in the Sun's atmosphere for weeks or sometimes months.

More about the Sun

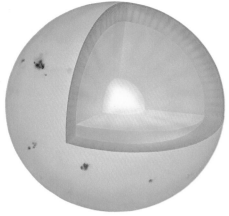

In the Sun's core the temperature is so high that nuclear reactions take place. These reactions convert more than 4 million tons of matter into energy every second. This energy flows outward to the Sun's surface and then escapes into space.

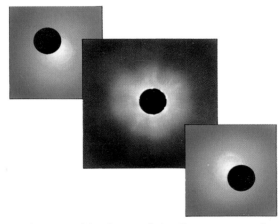

An eclipse, or blocking, of the Sun occurs when the Moon passes between the Sun and the Earth. During a total eclipse, the Sun is completely covered and only the corona — the Sun's faint outer atmosphere — can be seen.

People were once afraid of eclipses. Long ago the Chinese thought that an eclipse was caused by a dragon trying to swallow the Sun. When an eclipse occurred, the people would make a lot of noise to frighten the dragon away!

More about stars

How big are stars?

Stars differ enormously in size. Red giants and supergiants are huge, cool stars, often a hundred times larger than the Sun. The Sun itself is more than a hundred times bigger than a tiny, hot white dwarf star. A typical white dwarf star is about the same size as the Earth.

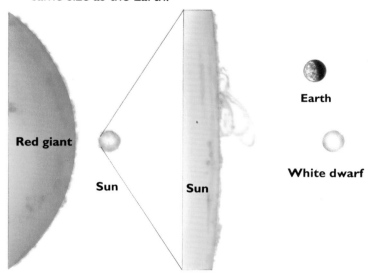

Red giant

Sun

Sun

Earth

White dwarf

How do you find stars from the Great Bear?

Seven of the Great Bear's — Ursa Major's — stars *(right)* make up the shape of a saucepan with a bent handle. This is known as the Big Dipper, or the Plow. Two stars, Merak and Dubhe, are known as the Pointers. A line drawn through them leads to Polaris, the Pole Star.

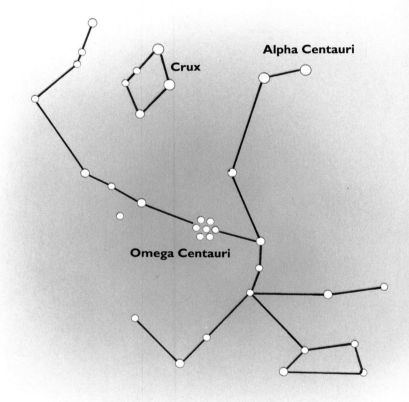

Crux

Alpha Centauri

Omega Centauri

How big is Betelgeuse?

Betelgeuse, in Orion, is an immense star. If it was placed at the center of the Solar System, the Sun, Mercury, Venus, Earth, and Mars would all fit inside.

How do you find stars from Orion?

Orion, the Hunter *(right)*, is a beautiful constellation, or pattern of stars, best seen in the winter sky. It includes 2 very bright stars: red Betelgeuse and blue-white Rigel. The line of Orion's "belt" (the 3 stars in the middle) leads down to Sirius, the Dog Star, the brightest star in the sky. Orion is a useful key to locating many other constellations.

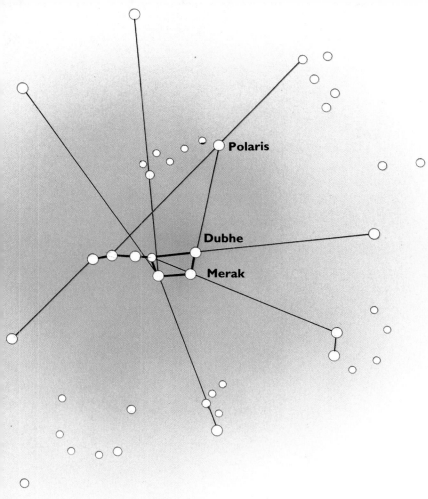

Polaris

Dubhe

Merak

How many stars are there in Orion?
The constellation of Orion includes 7 bright stars. Although these stars seem quite close together in the sky, they are actually located at different distances from the Earth. For example, Rigel is nearly three times as distant from us as Betelgeuse, and Mintaka is more than twice as far as Rigel.

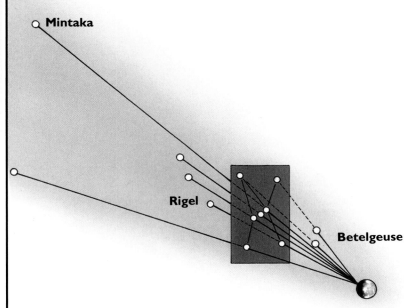

Mintaka

Rigel

Betelgeuse

What is Centaurus?
Centaurus *(left)* is a brilliant constellation visible in the Southern Hemisphere. Alpha Centauri, the brightest star in the constellation, is the nearest star that can be seen without a telescope. Omega Centauri is a magnificent star cluster. Nearby is Crux, the Southern Cross.

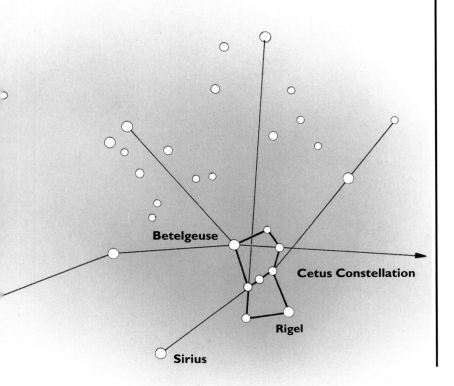

Betelgeuse

Cetus Constellation

Rigel

Sirius

What are the signs of the zodiac?
The zodiac is the band of sky where the Sun, Moon, and planets are located. Twelve main "signs," or constellations, are in the zodiac: Aries, Taurus, Gemini, Cancer, Leo, Virgo, Libra, Scorpius, Sagittarius, Capricornus, Aquarius, and Pisces.

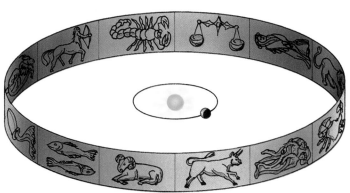

How did the universe begin?

Most astronomers believe that the universe began in a hot, dense explosion, called the Big Bang, which occurred between 10 and 20 billion years ago. As the universe expanded, its hot material cooled down. Eventually huge clumps of gases were able to form into galaxies. Within each galaxy, smaller clumps of gases turned into stars. Then planets were formed around the stars. Even today the galaxies are still rushing away from each other because of the violence of the original explosion from which the universe was born.

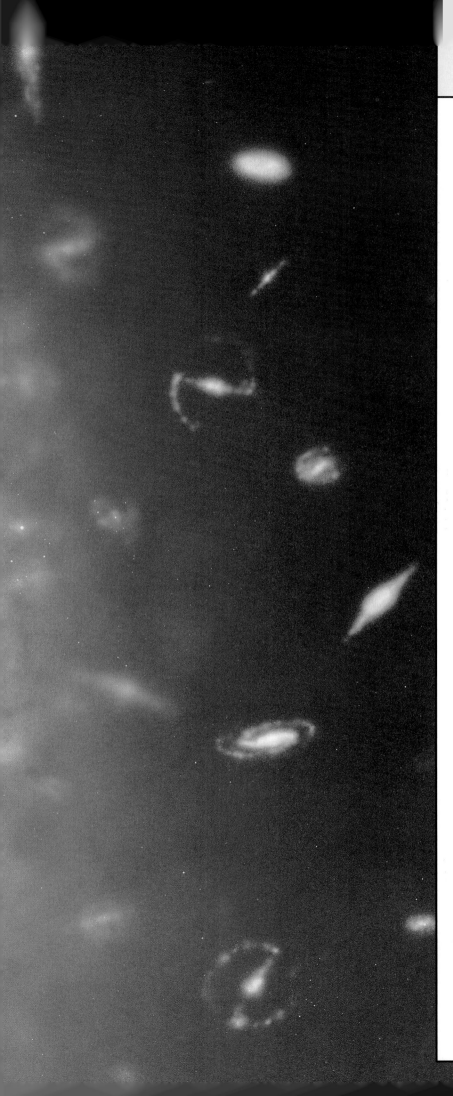

How the Solar System began

Nearly 5 billion years ago, a cloud of gases inside our galaxy began to collapse on itself because of the pull of gravity. As it collapsed, it began to spin faster, eventually forming a spinning disk. The central part of the disk grew hotter and denser and finally became the Sun.

Inside the swirling disk, small particles of solid matter began to form. These stuck together to make bigger lumps, which collided with each other and formed planets, like the Earth. The giant planets, such as Jupiter, were formed mainly from gases.

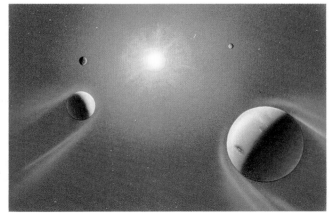

Ultimately, as the Sun became hot and bright, the remaining gases and dust blew away, leaving the Solar System as it is today.

What are comets?

Comets are remnants of material left over from the formation of the Solar System. The main part of a comet is a lump of ice and dust, called the nucleus, that moves around the Sun along an elliptical, or oval, path. The nucleus is only a few miles in diameter. Each time the comet approaches the Sun, gases and dust are driven from the nucleus to form a huge cloud called the comet's head, or coma, and a tail. Halley's comet was named after the English astronomer Edmond Halley, who first proved that comets, which travel around the Sun, return periodically. When this comet made its most recent approach in 1986, the European spacecraft *Giotto* passed within 373 miles of the comet's nucleus and sent detailed pictures back to Earth.

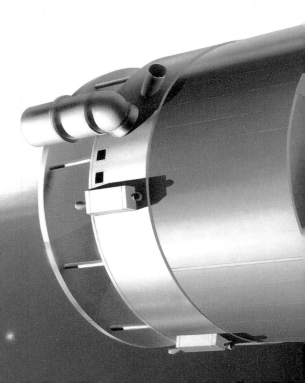

More about comets

People used to think that when a comet appeared, it was an omen that something terrible was going to happen. This tapestry, in Bayeux, France, shows Halley's comet, which appeared in 1066 before the Battle of Hastings. King Harold of England was killed in the battle by the invading Norman army.

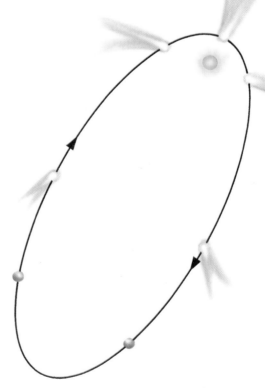

When a comet is far from the Sun, it has no tail. The tail begins to grow when the comet approaches the Sun and shrinks again when it recedes. The tail always points away from the Sun.

Why do auroras glow?

Auroras are shimmering patterns of faintly colored light that appear when atomic particles from the Sun collide with the thin gases of the upper atmosphere. Sometimes auroras appear as a shapeless glow, but at other times they take the form of bands, rays, curtains, or curving arches of light that brighten, fade, and show rapid changes of shape. Greens and reds and whites are common shades, but yellows and blues might also be seen. Auroral displays are often called the Northern Lights (Aurora Borealis) or Southern Lights (Aurora Australis).

More about auroras

Views from space show that displays of auroras usually occur in oval bands around the Earth's North or South poles. Auroras occur at heights of between 60 and 600 miles above the ground.

The solar wind is a stream of atomic particles (electrons and protons) that flows from the Sun and blows past the Earth at speeds of around 300 miles per second. The Earth's magnetic field deflects most of these particles away from our planet. However, some particles can flow into the atmosphere near the poles, especially after a big eruption, called a solar flare, on the Sun. These captured particles cause auroras.

How does the Hubble Space Telescope work?

The Hubble Space Telescope, named after the American astronomer Edwin Hubble, is the largest optical, or visible light, telescope ever to be put into space. It is a reflecting telescope, 42 feet long, that uses a mirror almost 8 feet in diameter to collect light and feed it to a range of instruments. The information received is beamed back to Earth by radio. Launched in April 1990, this telescope orbits the Earth at a height of about 404 miles. At this distance, it clears the atmosphere and has a better view of the universe than Earth-based telescopes.

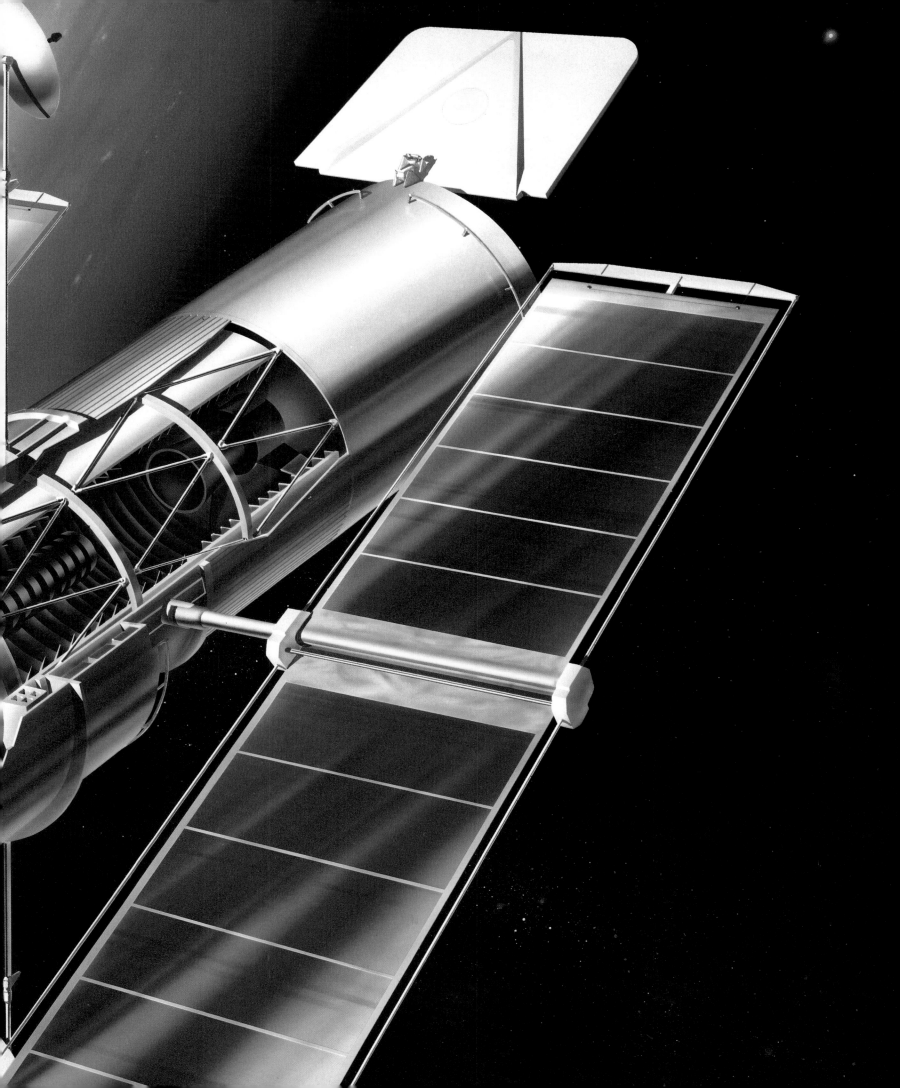

More about telescopes

Why was Galileo so important?

The telescope was adapted for astronomical use by Galileo Galilei in Florence, Italy, in about 1610. Galileo saw mountains and craters on the Moon, discovered 4 moons around the planet Jupiter, and saw that the Milky Way was made up of vast numbers of stars.

What does a radio telescope do?

Many distant objects in space give out radio waves. A radio telescope collects these waves, often using a huge dish like this one, so that astronomers can study the objects. The largest steerable radio dish is 325 feet across and is located in Germany.

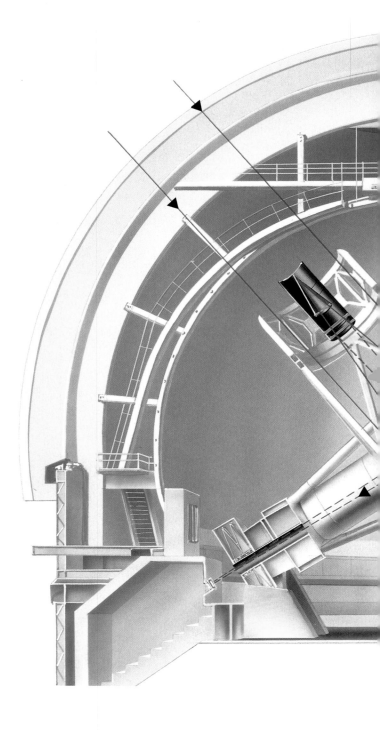

Why are observatories built on high mountain sites?

The Earth's atmosphere is dusty, unsteady, and often cloudy. Large observatories are usually built high up on mountains so that their telescopes can get a clearer view from above many of the clouds and denser parts of the atmosphere.

What is an observatory?

An observatory is a building that contains a large telescope. Its roof is usually a dome with a slot that can be opened. The dome can also rotate to allow the telescope to look at different parts of the sky. Observatories also have special equipment to study the light collected by the telescope.

What is the Keck Telescope?

The Keck Telescope is a huge telescope located on top of a high mountain in Hawaii. Its main mirror, which consists of 36 separate segments, is $32\frac{1}{2}$ feet across. It was made this way because it is easier to make many smaller segments than to make a single large mirror.

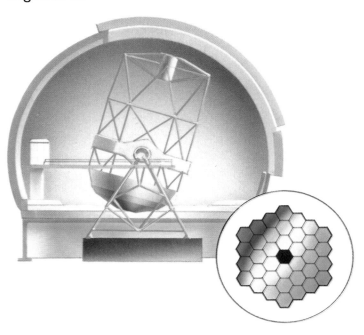

What is the William Herschel Telescope?

The William Herschel Telescope, named after the astronomer who discovered the planet Uranus, is a powerful reflecting telescope with a main mirror that is 14 feet in diameter. It is located on La Palma Island in the Canary Islands.

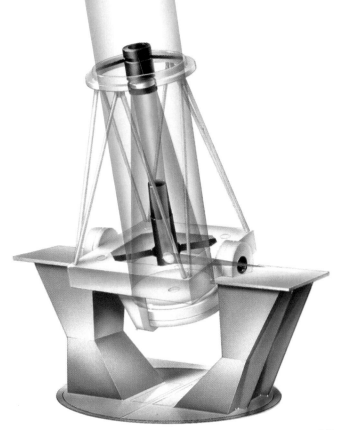

What is the surface of Venus like?

Venus is a very hostile world. Its dense atmosphere, which is composed mainly of carbon dioxide gas, is so heavy that it would crush any astronaut who might step onto the planet's surface. The atmosphere acts like a blanket to keep the surface temperature at 900°F.—hot enough to melt lead. Most of the surface consists of undulating plains, but there are high mountains, deep valleys, and shallow craters, too. Venus also has a number of volcanoes, some of which may be active, pouring out lava, like the one seen here. Scientists believe that flashes of lightning may sometimes light up its gloomy cloud-laden sky.

More about planet surfaces

Seen from space, the Earth *(top)* and Venus *(bottom)* look very different. The Earth is partly covered with clouds, but large areas of ocean and land can easily be seen from space. Venus is completely covered with thick yellowish clouds that are composed of tiny droplets of sulfuric acid.

The rocky surface of Mercury *(top)* is covered with craters. At noon its temperature is extremely high, but since it has no air to hold in heat, its surface becomes very cold at night. Tiny Pluto *(bottom)*, is usually the most distant planet. It is always extremely cold. Its frozen, icy surface may look like this.

How big is Jupiter?

With a diameter of 88,850 miles, Jupiter is the largest planet of all. Eleven Earths in a row would barely stretch from one side of Jupiter to the other. Despite its huge size, Jupiter rotates in just 9 hours and 50 minutes—a shorter rotation period than any other planet. Its clouds form colorful belts and zones that stretch all the way around the planet. A major feature is the Great Red Spot, a swirling, reddish-colored weather system, or storm, that has lasted for 300 years or longer. Jupiter has 4 large moons and a dozen small ones. Two of the large ones are shown here: Io and *(in the foreground)* Europa.

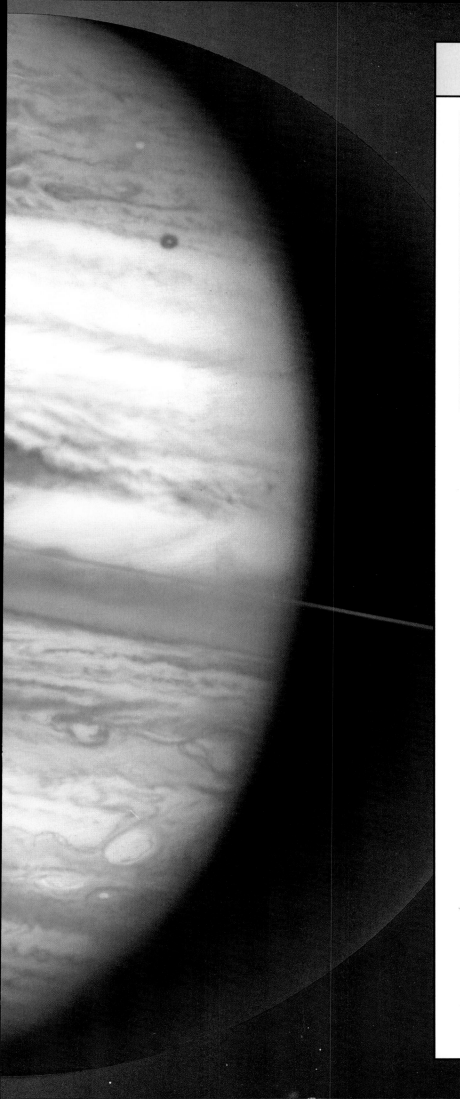

More about Jupiter

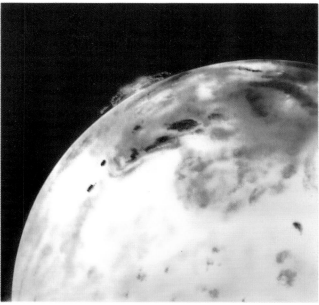

Io, the innermost of Jupiter's large satellites, is about the same size as the Earth's Moon. Its orange-yellow surface is covered with sulfur thrown out from violently active volcanoes, which hurl material as high as 200 miles.

Launched in October 1989, the *Galileo* spacecraft should reach Jupiter in December 1995. If all goes according to plan, it will go into orbit around Jupiter and begin a 22-month study of the planet and its moons. It will also release a probe that will plunge deep into Jupiter's cloudy atmosphere. However, scientists will not be able to receive information from the spacecraft unless problems with its defective antenna are corrected.

How wide are Saturn's rings?

Saturn, the second-largest planet, is surrounded by a beautiful system of rings, which can easily be seen with a small telescope. The main rings are about 170,000 miles across, a distance which is more than two thirds of the distance from the Earth to the Moon. Like Jupiter, Saturn is composed mainly of hydrogen gas and has no solid surface. Its cloud-covered globe spins around in 10 hours and 39 minutes, so fast that the planet bulges out at its equator. Saturn is 886.7 million miles from the Sun — nearly ten times farther than the Earth is — and takes nearly 30 years to travel once around the Sun.

More about Saturn

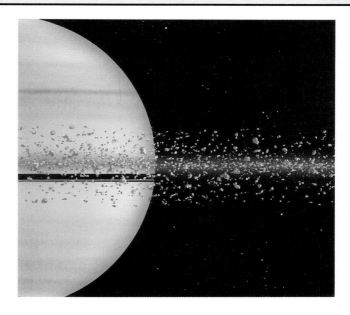

Saturn's rings are made up of millions of pieces of rock and ice. These range in size from tiny particles of dust to lumps as big as cars or small houses.

Because of the way in which Saturn and its rings are tilted, their appearance, as seen from Earth, changes as the planet travels around the Sun. Every 14 or 15 years, the rings are edge-on to us and are invisible for many months. At other times we see either the north or the south face of the rings.

What does Neptune look like?

Neptune, which has a diameter four times greater than the Earth's, is the farthest of the giant planets from the Sun. It takes nearly 165 years to complete each lonely orbit of the Sun. Its hazy blue atmosphere contains bands of cloud and a Great Dark Spot similar to the Great Red Spot on Jupiter. A few bright clouds float high above the main cloud layers. Neptune has 4 faint rings, seen edge-on in this view. Triton, seen here, is by far the largest of Neptune's 8 moons. It has a thin atmosphere, a frozen, icy surface, and is the coldest place known in the Solar System.

More about planets

Why is Copernicus famous?

People used to believe that the Earth was the center of the universe and that the Sun, planets, and stars traveled around the Earth. Nicolaus Copernicus (1473–1543) was a Polish astronomer who had a different idea. He proposed, correctly, that the Earth and planets travel around the Sun.

What is strange about Pluto's orbit?

Pluto is the most distant planet — for most of the time. It takes nearly 248 years to travel around its orbit but spends 20 of those years inside the orbit of Neptune. Pluto is inside Neptune's orbit now and will be the eighth planet from the Sun through the 1990s. Each time the two planets' orbits cross, Pluto passes above the orbit of Neptune, so there is no danger of the planets colliding.

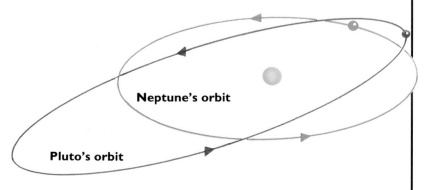

Neptune's orbit

Pluto's orbit

What is it like inside the Earth?

The innermost part of the Earth (below) is called the core. The solid inner core is surrounded by the outer core. This is very hot and consists mainly of liquid metals, such as iron and nickel. The outer core is surrounded by a deep layer of dense rocks, called the mantle. On top of the mantle is a thin crust of lighter rocks.

EARTH

MERCURY

What is it like inside Jupiter?

The atmosphere around Jupiter *(below)* is about 600 miles thick and is made up mainly of hydrogen and helium gases. It merges into an ocean of liquid hydrogen at least 12,000 miles deep. This lies on top of a liquid, metallic hydrogen layer more than 25,000 miles deep. A core of rocks and metals makes up the center of the planet.

JUPITER

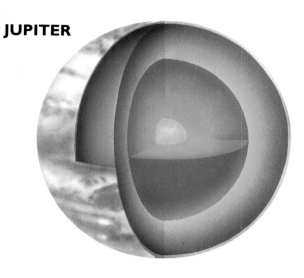

What is it like inside Uranus?

Uranus *(below)* has a deep, cold, and hazy atmosphere made up mainly of hydrogen and helium gases together with other gases, such as methane. The atmosphere merges into a deep layer of slushy ice. The center of the planet probably contains a core of rocks and minerals.

URANUS

What is it like inside Mercury?

Most of the inside of Mercury *(left)* is made up of a metallic core about 2,200 miles in diameter. This is surrounded by a layer of dense rocks and a crust of lighter rocks.

What is Gaspra?

On October 29, 1991, the *Galileo* spacecraft flew within 1,000 miles of a tiny asteroid called Gaspra. The first picture that was sent back showed that Gaspra has an irregular shape and is covered with craters.

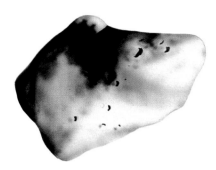

What happens when asteroids collide?

Asteroids are small bodies that travel around the Sun. Collisions between asteroids produce fragments, called meteoroids, which plunge through the atmosphere from time to time and strike the Earth's surface.

What might Titan's surface look like?

The surface of Saturn's giant moon, Titan, may be covered by oceans of liquid methane. Cliffs and mountains of ice may rise up toward the methane clouds that hang in the hazy, orange-tinted sky.

What is a Lunar Rover?

Between 1969 and 1972, six American Apollo missions landed successfully on the Moon. Each spacecraft consisted of a Command Module and a Lunar Module *(seen in the background)*. The Command Module remained in orbit around the Moon with one astronaut aboard, and the Lunar Module took two astronauts down to the surface. The final three missions also carried a battery-powered car — the Lunar Rover — that allowed the astronauts to explore up to 5 miles from the landing site. Since there is no air on the Moon, astronauts must wear spacesuits at all times. The astronauts' footprints can be seen on the Moon's dusty surface, and the Earth shines bright in the black lunar sky.

More about moon landings

The Saturn V, which was used to launch Apollo spacecraft, was the most powerful rocket ever built in the United States. It consisted of three sections, or stages, stacked one on top of the other. One by one, each section dropped off when its fuel was used up. With an Apollo spacecraft mounted on top, Saturn V stood 363 feet tall and weighed about 2,900 tons.

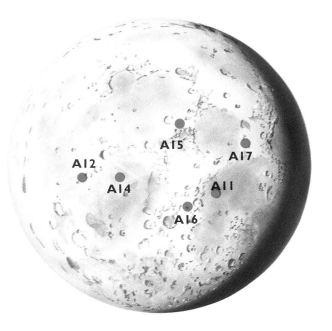

This map shows the main dark plains (although there is no water on the Moon, these areas are called "seas" on maps) and bright highland areas on the Moon. The landing sites of *Apollos 11, 12, 14, 15, 16,* and *17* are shown. *Apollo 11* made the first manned landing on July 20, 1969, and *Apollo 17* made the last on December 7, 1972.

Which planets did *Voyager 2* visit?

Unmanned spacecraft have visited every planet in the Solar System except Pluto. However, *Voyager 2* is the only one to have flown past all 4 of the giant planets. Uranus, seen here with *Voyager 2*, is four times the size of Earth and has a deep, hazy atmosphere with faint belts of cloud. It has 15 moons, 10 of which were discovered by *Voyager 2*, and 11 narrow rings. *Voyager 2* carries many instruments, including cameras, and has a communications dish 12 feet across that is used to receive instructions from Earth. *Voyager 2*, which was launched in 1977, is now well beyond Neptune and is heading out toward the stars—never to return.

More about *Voyager 2*'s journey

Only 292 miles in diameter, Miranda is the strangest moon of Uranus. Its icy surface is covered with craters, valleys, high cliffs, and irregular grooves and streaks. Some astronomers think that, long ago, Miranda may have broken up and then come together again in a mixed-up, disorderly way.

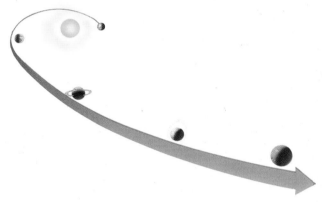

Since the giant planets were lined up in a special way, which will not happen again for about 180 years, *Voyager 2* was able to fly past Jupiter, Saturn, Uranus, and Neptune on a single mission. It reached Neptune, 2,700 million miles from Earth, in 1989, having taken only 12 years to get there.

Just in case it is ever found by intelligent aliens, *Voyager 2* carries a long-playing record containing images and sounds of the Earth and its life-forms. Symbols on the record's case show where the Earth is located.

What will it be like to land on Mars?

Imagine the first manned expedition touching down on Mars. The parachutes, which help to slow the spacecraft as it comes down through the planet's thin atmosphere, are drifting away. In the distance are the gentle slopes of a giant, extinct volcano, Olympus Mons, whose summit is more than 15 miles high. The sky color can change from pink to orange because the air is full of dust, whipped up by strong winds that often blow across the planet's dusty, boulder-strewn surface. Manned missions to Mars are likely to begin in the twenty-first century as a first step toward setting up a permanent base and, perhaps, the eventual colonization of the planet.

More about space travel

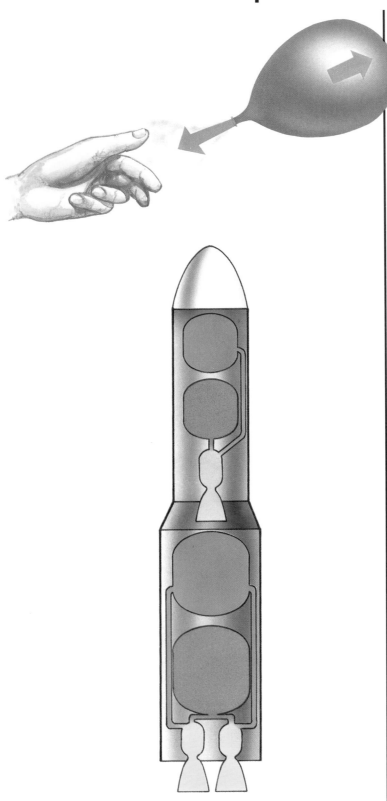

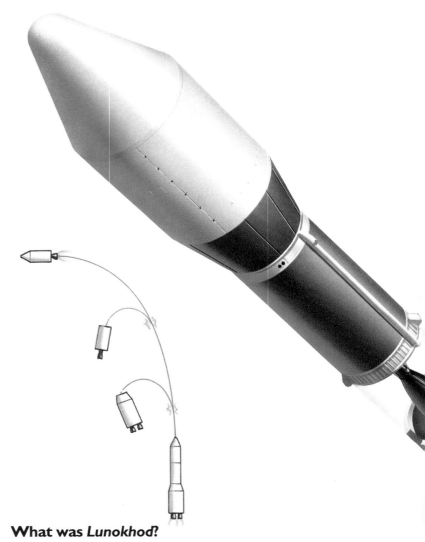

What was *Lunokhod*?

Lunokhod was a Soviet remote-controlled vehicle that landed on the surface of the Moon in 1970. It could carry television cameras and various other instruments. Although it looked like a mobile bathtub, it was a very successful vehicle. *Lunokhod* explored the lunar surface for about 11 months.

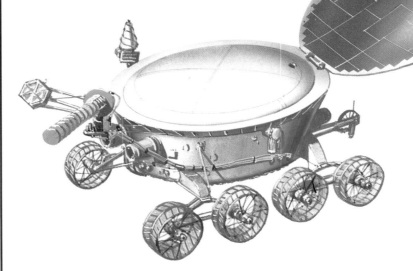

How does a rocket work?

A liquid-fueled rocket burns a mixture of fuel and oxidant (a chemical that contains oxygen) in its combustion chamber. As the hot gases escape from its nozzle, the rocket is pushed in the opposite direction, just as an inflated balloon rushes away when the inside air is released.

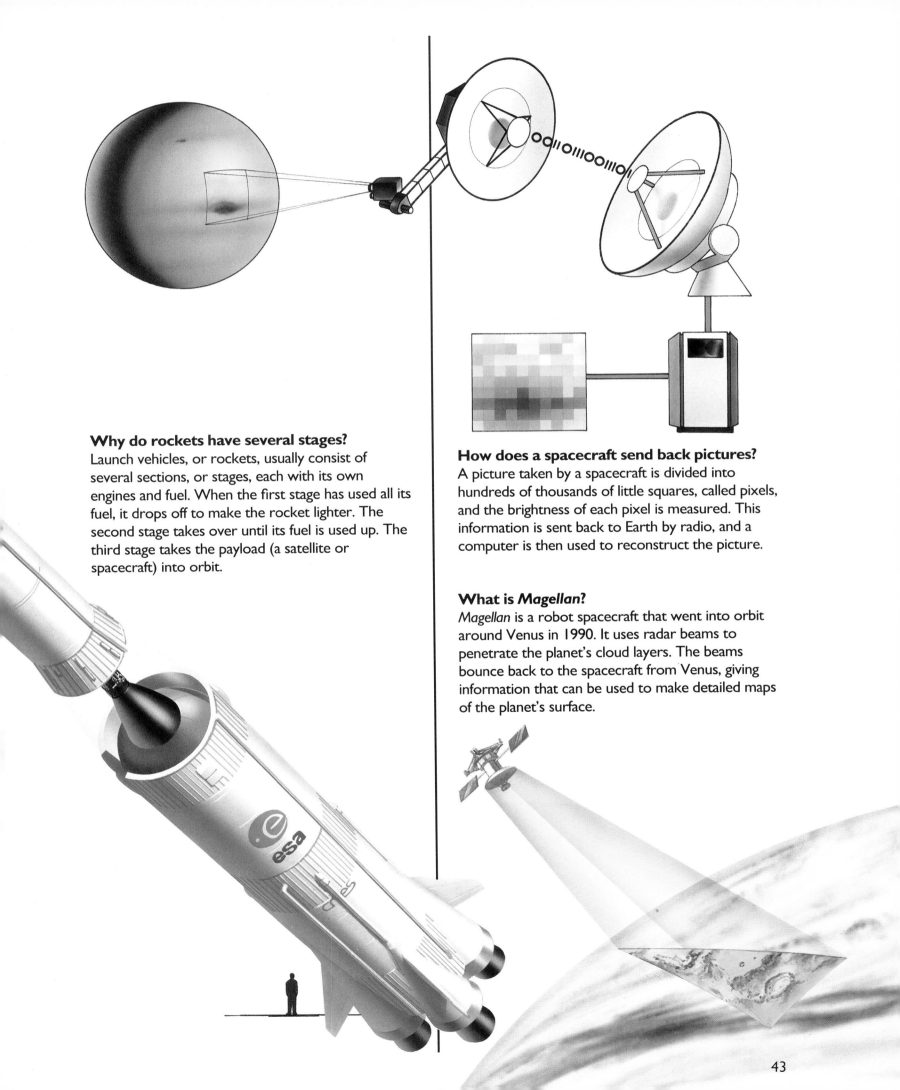

Why do rockets have several stages?

Launch vehicles, or rockets, usually consist of several sections, or stages, each with its own engines and fuel. When the first stage has used all its fuel, it drops off to make the rocket lighter. The second stage takes over until its fuel is used up. The third stage takes the payload (a satellite or spacecraft) into orbit.

How does a spacecraft send back pictures?

A picture taken by a spacecraft is divided into hundreds of thousands of little squares, called pixels, and the brightness of each pixel is measured. This information is sent back to Earth by radio, and a computer is then used to reconstruct the picture.

What is *Magellan*?

Magellan is a robot spacecraft that went into orbit around Venus in 1990. It uses radar beams to penetrate the planet's cloud layers. The beams bounce back to the spacecraft from Venus, giving information that can be used to make detailed maps of the planet's surface.

43

How does the Space Shuttle work?

The Space Shuttle is a reusable winged spacecraft that is launched vertically, like a rocket, but which lands on a runway like an airplane. Behind the crew compartment is a payload bay, about 60 feet long and 15 feet wide, shown here with its doors fully open. Its cargoes have included satellites, unmanned spacecraft, and a manned laboratory called Spacelab. A remote-controlled arm is used to lift satellites and spacecraft out of the payload bay and to release them into space. Astronauts can travel short distances from the Shuttle by using a backpack powered by tiny rockets, which is known as the Manned Maneuvering Unit.

More about the Space Shuttle

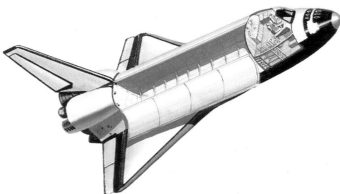

The crew compartment has two decks: a flight deck and a middeck. The flight deck carries the commander, the pilot, and 2 flight engineers, while the middeck has seating for additional engineers and scientists. An airlock leads to the payload bay. As many as 8 people at a time can fly in the Space Shuttle.

At launch, the Shuttle Orbiter is attached to a huge external tank, which carries most of the fuel for its main engines. Two powerful, solid-fueled boosters assist the lift off, then drop off about 2 minutes into the flight. The external tank falls away about 6 minutes later.

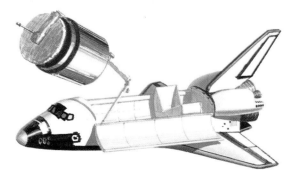

The remote-controlled arm has lifted this satellite clear of the payload bay and is about to release it into space. A small rocket engine attached to the satellite will then boost it up to a higher orbit.

Index

AN ILEX BOOK
Created and produced by Ilex Publishers Limited
29-31 George Street, Oxford, OX1 2AY

Main illustrations by Sebastian Quigley/Linden Artists